I KNEW YOU COULD!

CELEBRATE ALL THE STOPS IN YOUR LIFE

Library of Congress Cataloging-in-Publication Data

Dorfman, Craig.
I knew you could! / by Craig Dorfman ; illustrated by Cristina Ong.
p. cm.
Summary: "The Little Engine That Could" advises how to find one's
own track, handle life's ups and downs, and even face
the dark tunnels that can make one frightened or sad.
[1. Railroads–Trains–Fiction. 2. Self-reliance–Fiction. 3. Stories
in rhyme.] I. Ong, Cristina, ill. II. Title.
PZ8.3.D734Iae 2003
[Fic]–dc21
2002014375

ISBN 978-0-448-44813-8   10 9 8 7 6 5 4 3 2 1

I KNEW YOU COULD!

CELEBRATE ALL THE STOPS IN YOUR LIFE

written by CRAIG DORFMAN • illustrated by CRISTINA ONG

GROSSET & DUNLAP • NEW YORK

To:

From:

I knew you could! And you knew it, too—

That you'd come out on top after all you've been through.

And from here you'll go farther and see brand-new sights.

You'll face brand-new hills that rise to new heights.

I wish I could show you the stops that you'll visit,

But that isn't my choice to make for you, is it?

Instead, I can tell you some lessons and tales

That I've learned and relearned in my time on the rails.

First of all, you must find your own track,

So you can start right away and not be held back

But which track is yours? Well, that all depends

On which way it's going and where it might end.

Different tracks wind around,

over, under, and through,

So pick out the one

that works best for you.

Though the track you start out on

will feel like "the one,"

You might take a few more before you are done.

And now, with your eyes on your new destination,

Start up your wheels and roll out of the station.

On your new trip, you'll make plenty of stops,

In deep river valleys and on high mountaintops.

Some will surprise you and some will be planned,

And you'll roll through each one saying, *"I think I can!"*

You'll go through tunnels, surrounded by dark,

And you'll wish for a light or even a spark.

You might get scared or a little bit sad,

Wondering if maybe your track has gone bad.

So here's some advice to help ease your doubt:

The track you took in must also go out.

So steady yourself and just keep on going—

Before you know it, some light will be showing.

And then you'll be out, heading to a new place.

You'll be ready for the next tunnel you face.

Sometimes you'll look up and see planes in the sky,

And you'll think to yourself, "I wish *I* could fly."

The cars on the roads will seem quick and free—

You'll feel stuck on your track and think, "I wish that were me."

But the plane might wish he could get out of the air,

Saying, "I wish I could travel like that train down there."

The cars will watch as you speed right along,

And they'll say to each other,

"Look how fast and how strong!"

Don't worry about not being a car or a plane,

Just enjoy the trip you'll take as a train.

Don't be afraid to toot your own horn,

If you need to be heard or there are people to warn.

Or if being yourself just makes you so proud

That you want to share it and sing it out loud.

You'll follow your track

through twists and through bends,

And stop at new stops and pick up new friends.

They'll all come aboard with smiles and greetings.

You'll have such great times

with the people you're meeting.

On the days when you're sad and feel you can't go,

Speak up and ask a friend for a tow.

That's what friends do, so don't be afraid.

You'd do the same if your friend needed aid.

You might stop at some stops that you never have toured,

And look for new friends, but they won't come aboard.

So you'll have to head out with a creak and a groan,

Setting out once again on your track, all alone.

Try to remember that the world is so wide,

Full of all kinds of people with their own trains to ride.

Just stay true to yourself as you travel your track,

With no second-guessing and no looking back.

Once you're on the right track, you'll probably say,
"This one is mine—I'm here to stay."
Try to enjoy the track that you choose—
Stop now and then to take in the views.

I THINK I CAN!

If you rush forward, as a general rule,

Before you arrive, you could run out of fuel.

Don't overwork, but save up some strength.

That way, every day, you can travel great lengths.

You'll need all that strength on the days when you're stuck,
Or tired, or sad, or just out of luck.

When your belief in yourself doesn't feel quite so pure,

And your "I think I can" doesn't sound quite so sure,

That's when to push and to strive and to strain,

To show the world you're not a giving-up train.

And you're wise if you know that doing your best

Means that sometimes you should just slow down and rest.

Speeding through your whole trip will bring only sorrow,

So slow down today to be happy tomorrow.

There's more about life that you'll learn as you go,

Because figuring things out on your own helps you grow.

Just trust in yourself, and you'll climb every hill.

Say, *"I think I can!"* and you know what?

You will!